Baden-Powell

CHIEF SCOUT OF THE WORLD

JOHN GELINAS JR.

Copyright © 2019 John Gelinas Jr.

ISBN: 978-1-6847-0083-7 (sc)
ISBN: 978-1-6847-0082-0 (e)

Andrew John Thomas Gelinas, Editor

The linocut images in this book are the author/illustrator's representations of Baden-Powell's drawings, which are the property of The Scout Association (UK), and are reproduced with permission of The Scout Association, Heritage Service.

Lulu Publishing Services rev. date: 07/10/2019
First Edition

For my wife,
my mother,
my children,
my brothers and sisters, and
my Scouting friends and family.

And in memory of my father.

CONTENTS

INTRODUCTION

Scouting!

For more than a century, hundreds of millions of young people all over the world have grown up as Scouts.

Scouts help other people and serve their communities. They are patriots and citizens loyal to their nations. They camp and hike in the outdoors.

Scouts promise to do their best to keep their bodies strong, and their minds sharp. They do their best to do what is right. Some Scouts even save other people's lives. Today, millions of people are alive, all over the world, because of Scouts who saved them or saved their parents or grandparents.

Scouting! One man started it all.

Robert Baden-Powell

Robert Baden-Powell of England had the idea of Scouting, and started the movement that today includes over 30 million boys and girls in over 200 countries.

Before he started Scouting, Baden-Powell was a war hero in England. He and his record of captivating military feats while he served in the British Army were famous around the world. And after he had retired from military service, he became even more famous as the founder of Scouting, and later as the Chief Scout of the World.

CHAPTER 1

EARLY YEARS

Robert Stephenson Smyth Powell was born in Paddington in Central London, England on February 22, 1857. His family called him, "Stephe," which sounded like, "Stevie." His father, Reverend Professor Baden Powell ("Baden" was his first name), was an amateur astronomer, a college mathematics teacher, and a clergyman in the Church of England. His mother, Henrietta Grace Smyth, was 28 years younger than his father. Robert had five brothers and one sister.

When Robert was three years old, his father died. His mother raised him and his siblings, and taught them to love adventure, and to be honorable and self-reliant.

When he was eight years old, Robert wrote a set of rules for himself that he called, "Rules for me when I am old." Those rules included praying to God, and trying "very hard to be good."

When he was 12, his mother changed the family's last name from Powell to Baden-Powell to honor her husband, and Robert became Robert Baden-Powell. His friends called him, "BP."

BP grew up playing with his siblings in a London city park called Hyde Park. On nearby rivers, he and his brothers sought adventure. They loved exploring nature and the outdoors. They sailed boats, worked as a team, and became physically fit.

As a young boy and teenager, BP wrote and acted in plays, read, sang, and played musical instruments (including the violin, flugelhorn, and bugle). He drew sketches and he painted with both hands. Yes, he was ambidextrous. He played goalie on his school's football team (which is called soccer in America). He started a high school rifle corps. He was cheerful, and he liked to make people smile and laugh.

BP was very popular among his classmates, but he did not have any very close friends. He spent a lot of time alone. He liked pretending that he lived in the woods. He liked tracking and sneaking up on small animals, including rabbits, squirrels, rats, and birds, in order to observe them.

Sometimes in school, BP ranked last in his class. His grades were low, but he was not lazy. No. He had a lot of energy. He had so many activities that he had little time for schoolwork. When he was 19, BP applied for admission to become a student at Oxford – one of England's most famous and best universities. Years before, BP's father had been a professor at Oxford, and his older brothers had been honor students there. Though he did his best, BP was not accepted to Oxford. He and his family were disappointed.

Instead of going to college, BP decided he wanted to join the British Army. The British Military had been famous for hundreds of years, and its presence was known all over the world. BP's grandfather had been an admiral, and his uncle was an officer. BP studied very hard for his entrance examinations. When he got the results of his tests, he was excited, and his family was pleased. His grades were excellent, and he was able to become a professional soldier.

CHAPTER 2
AN ARMY SPY

In 1876, when he was 19 years old, BP joined the British Army. He shipped off to India, where he served as a soldier for eight years. He was a good soldier, and served as an intelligence officer. He went ahead of the other soldiers to explore the land. He watched the movements of the enemies, and he made drawings of their forts and positions. He served as a musketry teacher, a horseback riding instructor, a polo player, a theater director, and a manager of a musical band. He acted in plays, and he drew and painted.

In 1884, he wrote his first of more than 30 books. It was called *Reconnaissance and Scouting*. It was a guide to help soldiers explore the land, and to observe and spy on the enemy.

After serving in India, BP went to South Africa, at the tip of the African continent. There, the British Army struggled with the Boers (farmers of Dutch origin) who resented that the British ruled the country. The army also struggled with some of the native African tribes, including the Zulus.

BP was put in charge of spying missions in South Africa. He dressed up – almost like an actor in a play – and pretended to be just a simple man traveling with his horses on the plains and in the mountains. He said the best way to spy was to appear as if he belonged in the area. But secretly, he was observing and learning the secrets of the enemies.

He became so good at spying and gathering important information about Britain's enemies that the army later sent him to spy in Europe, including in Belgium, France, and Germany.

In 1888, BP returned to South Africa. At the time, there was a civil war between 13 Zulu tribal chiefdoms. BP served in many ways, and he became known as one of the best at giving first aid (First Aid is the help given to a wounded or sick person before complete medical treatment is available).

BP and his men chased the Zulus from their huts and forts. In some of the abandoned huts, BP and his men found weapons and trinkets. In one hut, BP found a long necklace of carved wooden beads that he thought had belonged to the Zulu chief Dinizulu. He kept it as a souvenir.

In 1890, when he was 33, BP returned to Europe. There, he continued to serve as an intelligence officer responsible for collecting important information about enemies. He was so clever. He pretended to be a fisherman, he dressed up like an eccentric artist, and he drew sketches of forts under foreign control. No one knew he was spying. The enemy thought that he just was fishing, drawing, or painting pictures of butterflies or mountains. He was an excellent spy.

One of BP's most famous spying adventures took place in Dalmatia, which was part of the powerful Austro-Hungarian Empire, and now part of the country of Croatia. There, BP collected information about a military fort at Cattaro.

BP dressed up like a butterfly hunter with a net and a bag. In disguise, as he hiked near the fort, he sketched pictures of butterflies. Hidden in the wings, he drew a map of the outline of the fort. On the edges of the wings, he marked the positions and sizes of the machine, fortress, and field guns stationed on the inside of the fort walls.

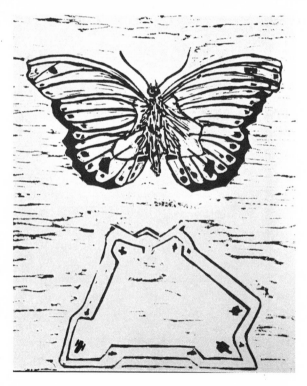

Butterfly and Fort

The outline of the fort and the positions of guns hidden within the wings of a drawing of a butterfly

BP returned to Africa where tribes were rebelling in the Second Matabele War in what was then called Rhodesia, and is now called The Republic of Zimbabwe. BP continued his work observing the landscape and spying on the enemy. Some Africans called him, "Impessa," which meant, "The wolf that never sleeps." BP played games of deception. For example, one time, he made hundreds of little campfires to fool the enemy tribes into thinking that there were hundreds of British soldiers nearby, when there were very few.

One day, BP found the twisted horn of a kudu, which is a type of antelope. The horn was a weapon of war used by the Matabele tribes. He kept it as souvenir. Also during that time, BP started wearing what would become his broad-brimmed campaign hat.

BP was a skillful soldier and spy. He loved adventure, and he was very brave. He was resourceful and cunning. He was alert, creative, and clever.

When he was 40 years old, he returned to India.

CHAPTER 3

THE BOER WAR

BP returned to South Africa when he was 42 years old. Another war had broken out. It became known as the Boer War, and lasted from 1899 to 1903.

BP was in charge of defending Mafeking, the largest town in the North Cape Colony. It was an important town. It had valuable railroad equipment, and was located in a strategic place. If the Boers were to capture the town, then other Boers would have been encouraged to join the fight against the British and to spread the war south. Mafeking had to be defended.

The Boers surrounded the town, and tried to capture it. BP was the soldier in charge of the town. He had to ration the food, so the citizens and other soldiers would not starve. He built shelters underground. He created special money and stamps so mail could be delivered in the town. He helped start a cadet corps of young boys (nine years old and up) to carry messages, deliver mail, help with first aid, and take turns at look-out posts. He tried to keep up the positive morale of the citizens by putting on plays. Everyone liked and respected BP. He was a good leader. He knew every soldier and every soldier's family. He was a leader with a personal touch.

BP fooled the Boers. He used his clever mind and experiences to make them think that there were many more British soldiers defending Mafeking than there really were, and he made them think they had many more weapons than they really had. He used his clever mind to bluff with boldness, and to use what he called, "Pluck and dash."

One day, BP had an idea. He had his soldiers put wooden posts in the ground surrounding the town. He pretended to connect the posts with barbed wires, and then he had his men act as if they were climbing carefully over and under the wires. The Boers watched from far away, and worried that if they were to attack the town, they first would have to get through the wire fence. But, it was a trick! Yes, there were posts, but there were no barbed wires connecting them.

Another time, BP fooled the Boers into thinking that the town was surrounded by mines placed inside wooden boxes. The boxes were marked by red flags so that townspeople would not get injured if they came too close. BP and his soldiers built hundreds of boxes, and placed them around the town. One day, he stuck a piece of dynamite into an anthill, and blew it up. That way, the Boers would see and assume that the mines were dangerous. But, it was another trick! There were no explosives inside the boxes.

After 217 days, the siege of Mafeking was over. More British soldiers – including BP's younger brother – came to rescue the people of the town, and to chase away the Boers.

BP was the hero of Mafeking. Once again, he had proven himself to be a strong and cunning leader with great self-control. He was the toast of England and the whole British Commonwealth. He received hundreds of letters from boys and girls, and he answered every one. He couldn't believe how popular he was.

After Mafeking, Queen Victoria of England promoted BP. When he was 43 years old, BP became the youngest Major-General in the British Army. Later, in 1907, he was promoted to Lieutenant General.

What is the British Commonwealth?

The United Kingdom is a group of countries under the sovereign rule of the King or Queen of England. Today, it is made up of the countries of England, Scotland, Wales, and Northern Ireland.

The British Commonwealth is a group of nations that feel an allegiance to Britain and the British Crown. Those countries include those of the United Kingdom, and many others that once were a part of the worldwide British Empire but that now make their own laws and govern themselves.

Those countries include Canada, Australia, Papua New Guinea, India, New Zealand, and South Africa, and more than forty others.

CHAPTER 4

POLICE INSPECTOR

After the war, BP stayed in South Africa. There, he became Inspector-General of the military police force. Once again, he was a popular leader. He had great energy. He got along with everyone. He was very organized, and he knew the land.

BP designed the police uniforms. They were comfortable, and included soft, khaki shirts, and broad-brimmed hats, called Boss of the Plains or BP hats.

BP gave the police a motto: "Be Prepared." This meant they were ready to take on any type of duty at any time.

The police units were divided into small patrols of six men. Patrols were organized into troops, and troops were organized into divisions. At each level, there were leaders in each unit.

CHAPTER 5
A BIG IDEA

In 1899, just before the siege of Mafeking, he had written a book called *Aids to Scouting* to train men for war. He wanted to train men to be self-reliant. It was a popular book in England.

After Mafeking, BP returned to England in 1903. There, he wrote a book to train boys for peace and citizenship.

BP wanted boys to use their senses to observe everything around them, and to understand and follow tracks. He wanted to help boys to enjoy a sense of adventure, to use their creativity, to become physically fit and strong, to use their clever minds to make observations and to sharpen their wits. He wanted them to learn about themselves by having fun through hiking, camping, observing, tracking, lighting fires with two matches, spending time around campfires, and practicing first aid. He wanted them to be active in doing good things. He wanted them to live with honor.

BP never talked down to young people. He took them seriously. He knew that if they were challenged and encouraged, they would rise up to complete any task. BP wanted boys to obey their elders and superiors, to be cheerful, and to be devoted to the God they worshipped. He wanted boys to be helpful to other people, and he charged them to do a "Good turn" every day.

BP wanted boys to develop strong character based on timeless values, and to strive to do their best. He wanted to form organizations of Scouts with patrols and troops, just as he had done in South Africa with the police force.

CHAPTER 6
CAMPING ON BROWNSEA ISLAND

To test his Scouting ideas, BP planned a camping trip. He invited 21 boys and his nine-year-old nephew Donald to Brownsea Island in Dorset, England for a week in August of 1907.

He organized the boys into four patrols named after animals – Bulls, Wolves, Ravens, and Curlews. Each patrol made its own flag. The four patrols made up a troop.

Every boy wore a fleur-de-lis Scout badge on his hat. The symbol represented the notion of a compass pointing to true north.

fleur-de-lis

The activities of each day began at dawn, as BP woke everyone up by blowing air through the spiral horn of an African kudu. It was the same horn he had found years before, during the Matabele rebellion.

After breakfast, the boys had a patriotic flag ceremony, said prayers, and then engaged in Scouting activities, including first aid and lifesaving drills, firemanship, mat weaving, martial arts, tug of war, and skills of observation and tracking animals.

The boys led the activities, and were supervised by adults. They learned and practiced Scoutcraft through the fun of games. They were encouraged always to do their best.

This was the first Scouting camping trip. It was a weekend of outdoor adventure, excitement, fellowship, and fun. It was a success.

CHAPTER 7

THE SCOUTING HANDBOOK

BP published *Scouting For Boys* on January 15, 1908. He wrote and he illustrated the book with his own sketches. It became known as the *Boy Scout Handbook*.

The handbook outlined the Scouting promise of adventure in the outdoors, and the learning of Scouting skills. It said that a Scout must act with honor and duty, to help other people at all times, and to be a good citizen. It said a Scout needs to use pluck, self-reliance, and discretion.

Scouting for Boys by BP

The handbook contained the Scout Promise or Oath, which Scouts recite. The Oath outlines a Scout's pledge to do his best to do his duty to his God, to his country, to other people, and to himself.

> **The Scout Oath**
>
> *On my honor, I will do my best*
> *to do my duty to God and my country*
> *and to obey the Scout Law;*
> *to help other people at all times;*
> *to keep myself physically strong,*
> *mentally awake,*
> *and morally straight.*

By reciting the Oath, a Scout is not promising to be perfect, and is not saying he will never make a mistake. Instead, a Scout is dedicating himself to doing the best he can in every situation.

OMHIWDMB:
On My Honor I Will Do My Best

The Scout Oath is not quaint. It is not old-fashioned. It is alive with elements essential for living a good life.

It is a bright beacon beaming with brilliant light. It shines a decency marking a way to a good life.

The handbook also contained the Scout Law. Each Scout was expected to study the twelve points of the Scout Law, and to vow to follow them.

The Twelve Points of the Scout Law

A Scout is:

Trustworthy
Loyal   Helpful
Friendly
Courteous   Kind
Obedient
Cheerful   Thrifty
Brave   Clean
Reverent

The meaning of each point is important to consider:

- *Trustworthy:* Tell the truth, and be known as one who tries hard to do so. Be honest.

- *Loyal:* Be a good friend, even in the harder times. Be steadfast. Hold tight to your friends, family, community, country, and God. Respect and remember what connects you to others. Agree to disagree; yet, strive always to find common ground.

✤ *Helpful:* Ease another's burden.

✤ *Friendly:* Smile, and be amiable. Say, "Hi, friend, good to see you."

✤ *Courteous:* Be polite. Be respectful. Be well mannered. Say, "Please," "Thank you," and, "I'm sorry."

✤ *Kind:* Be decent. Be thoughtful. Show you care. Treat others the way you want to be treated.

✤ *Obedient:* Follow the rules. Do your duty. Be amenable. Pay heed to laws and expectations; yet, work to change them if they are outdated or misguided.

✤ *Cheerful:* Show your gratitude for being alive by sporting a light countenance. Giggle. Laugh.

✤ *Thrifty:* Be prudent. Use your resources thoughtfully. Do not be wasteful. Do not borrow more than you can afford to repay. Save for tomorrow.

- *Brave:* Be courageous. Honor what you believe to be right. Be bold.

- *Clean:* Be virtuous. Strive towards purity of thought and deed.

- *Reverent:* Love and honor your God. Be devout. Be respectful.

The handbook also contained descriptions of the Scout salute and handshake. It described the parts of the Scout uniform. It said the Scout motto is, "Be Prepared," which was the very same motto that BP's police force in South Africa had adopted. It said the Scout slogan is, "Do a Good Turn Daily."

Later editions of the handbook included descriptions of Scout games, stories, observations, and instructions on getting to know animals and plants, tracking animals in the wild, camping, pioneering, pathfinding, tying knots, and signaling with flags and Morse Code. There were ideas about physical fitness, kindness, and chivalry, as well as first aid, lifesaving, citizenship, and reverence to God.

The book explained the various ranks that a boy could earn in Scouting. The highest rank at the time was King's Scout, in honor of Britain's ruler of the time, King George V.

BP's book was a big success. It was a bestseller. Boys and girls loved to read it. BP donated the money the book made to promote Scouting, so that the organization could grow, and more boys could learn about Scouting.

In the spring of 1910, BP retired from the military. He then devoted the rest of his life and his boundless energies to Scouting.

CHAPTER 8

SCOUTING SPREADS

Scouting became very popular in England. Then, it started spreading all over the world. Scout troops began to spring up across Europe, as well as in Chile, Brazil, Argentina, Australia, New Zealand, Canada, and the United States. Today, Scouting exists in over 200 countries.

An American named William D. Boyce brought Scouting to America. On a trip in 1909 to London, Boyce became lost in the dense fog, and a young Scout helped him to find his way. Boyce was so impressed with the boy that he decided to start Scouting in the United States.

In 1910, the Boy Scouts of America was founded. Boyce insisted that boys of all races and creeds be allowed to join. Its national leaders included Chief Scout Ernest Seton, National Scout Commissioner Dan Beard, and Chief Scout Executive James E. West.

BP's handbook, *Scouting for Boys*, was translated into many foreign languages.

Scouting For Boys, January 1908

Scouting spread to all corners of the world. A genuine brotherhood of Scouts from different countries, creeds, races, and religions was formed.

BP's mother and sister Agnes were enthusiastic about expanding Scouting to girls. Along with BP, they started a program for girls called Girl Guides.

In the United States, in 1912, BP's friend Juliette Gordon Low organized the American Girl Guides, which is now called Girl Scouts of the USA (GSUSA). More than 50 million American women alive today were Girl Scouts growing up. The organization is dedicated in its mission to help build girls of character, courage, and confidence so that they make the world a better place.

CHAPTER 9

MARRIAGE AND FAMILY

In 1912, when he was 55 years old, and two years after he had retired from the British Army, BP met Olave St. Clair Soames while on a sailing trip from England to the West Indies. The two fell in love, and were married later that same year in St. Peter's Church in Dorset, England.

They had three children: Peter, Heather, and Betty. They called their home near London, "Pax Hill." Pax in Latin means, "Peace." They named it in honor of the ending of the Great War (which later became known as World War I), and lived there for twenty happy years.

Olave and BP were an amazing couple. Together, they worked hard to spread Scouting around the world. They established other Scouting programs, too.

In 1916, the Wolf Cub Scouts was formed for younger boys. That same year, Olave became Chief Guide of Girl Guides.

Girl Guides

Soon after, Brownies was started for younger girls, and Senior Guides was started for older girls. Six years later, an organization for older Scouts was started. It was called Rover Scouts.

In the United States, some older Scouts – both boys and girls – became Explorers and others became Venturers. Exploring, which started in 1949, helps to introduce older teenagers to a variety of careers, and is organized around local BSA units called posts. Venturing, which started in 1998, supports older youth and young adults by encouraging their engagement in high adventure outdoor activities, and is organized around local BSA units called crews.

In its effort to promote Family Scouting, the Boy Scouts of America welcomed young girls into its Cub Scout program, beginning in 2018. The following year, the BSA welcomed girls aged 11 to 18 into its newly named program called, "Scouts BSA."

As BP wrote more than a hundred years ago, "Scouting is equally suited to boys and girls."

CHAPTER 10

TRAINING ADULT SCOUT LEADERS

BP recognized that while boys led their Scout patrols and troops, they needed adult supervision and guidance. He wanted Scout leaders to be well trained, so they could guide and encourage the young Scouts.

In 1919, a Scotsman named William de Bois Maclaren purchased 53 acres of land in Essex near London. He donated it to BP and the Scouting movement. It was named Gilwell. In September, 1919, the first Scoutmaster training course was held there.

The Scoutmasters were put into patrols, and the patrols functioned together in a troop named Troop 1.

At dawn each day, BP blew the kudu horn, the same one he had found during the Matabele rebellion, and the same one he had blown every morning during the first Boy Scout camping trip on Brownsea Island. The leaders took part in the same Scout activities as the boys they were supervising in their troops.

When they finished the training course, the leaders were given a token. Instead of a certificate or cloth badge, BP gave them wooden beads from the necklace he had found in the deserted African hut during the Zulu war in 1888. The course became known as Wood Badge, and has trained tens of thousands of adult Scout leaders around the world ever since.

Wood Badge beads and lanyard

CHAPTER 11

JAMBOREE!

In a spirit of peace and brotherhood following the end of the Great War, a cheerful and giant gathering of Scouts and Scout leaders took place in London in 1920. It was the first World Jamboree! There were 8,000 Scouts from 34 countries camping together for eight days. They competed in games, and displayed their Scouting skills. They sang, cheered, and celebrated around a host of campfires.

Campfires

At the closing ceremony, a boy from the audience yelled, "We, the Scouts of the world, salute you, Sir Robert Baden-Powell – Chief Scout of the World."

BP was surprised by the call. He replied, "…Let us go forth from here determined that we will develop among ourselves and our boys that comradeship, through the world-wide spirit of the Scout brotherhood, so that we may help to develop peace and happiness in the world and good will among men. Brother Scouts, answer me – will you join me in this endeavor?"

The crowd shouted together, in a sound as loud as thunder, "Yes!"

CHAPTER 12

LATER YEARS AND GOING HOME

BP wanted Scouting to produce young men and women of character. He did not want Scouting to be a military organization. He did not want Scouting to be political, or to oppose anyone's religious beliefs. He wanted it to benefit every young person's growth and development.

In 1929, King George the Fifth of Great Britain made BP a lord. BP chose the name of the Scout leader's training center as part of his official title. So, after that honor (one of many that they received), BP and Olave became Lord and Lady Robert Baden-Powell of Gilwell.

The fifth Scouting World Jamboree was held in Holland in 1937. There, BP addressed Scouts of all nations. He said, "The time has come for me to say good-bye....I want your lives to be happy and successful. You can make them so by doing your best to carry out the Scout Law all your days, whatever your station and wherever you are...."

Scouts of the world trying to pull BP back to the organization he founded.

In 1938, BP and Olave – Chief Scout and Chief Guide of the World – moved to a one-room cottage in Nyeri, Kenya in East Africa. There, they named their humble home Paxtu, as in Peace-2, their second peaceful and happy home. Also, in the East African language of Swahili, Paxtu, means, "Complete." At home, BP drew and sketched birds and animals and the landscape. He and Olave corresponded with their Scouting friends from all over the world.

Indeed, BP sought to bring peace and brotherhood to the world by leading young people, and in instilling them with Scout Spirit, as well as a sense of duty to God, country, other people, and themselves. He encouraged them to do their best (which is the Cub Scout motto), and to do a good turn daily (which is the Boy Scout slogan). He urged them to be strong in their bodies, to be sharp in their minds, and to live moral lives. He charged them to be cunning, and to be of good cheer.

On January 8, 1941, at the age of 83, BP passed away.

BP was a celebrated leader, soldier, and visionary. He was an artist, actor, and spy. He was a man of peace who promoted a worldwide brotherhood.

Lord Robert Baden-Powell of Gilwell was laid to rest in Nyeri, Kenya. His gravesite has been visited by tens of thousands of people from around the world. His gravestone is marked by a round circle inside a loop – a Scouting trail signal meaning, "Gone home."

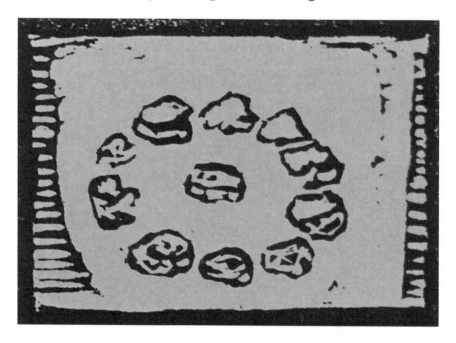

"Gone home."

BIBLIOGRAPHY

Baden-Powell, Robert; *Aids to Scouting*; Gale and Polden, Ltd.; London; 1915.

Baden-Powell, Robert; *My Adventures as a Spy*; C. Arthur Pearson, Ltd.; London; 1915.

Baden-Powell, Robert; *Scouting For Boys: A Handbook for Instruction in Good Citizenship*; Horace Cox; London; 1908.

Boy Scouts of America: The Official Handbook for Boys; Boy Scouts of America; New York, NY, USA; 1911.

Brower, Pauline York; *Baden-Powell: Founder of the Boy Scouts*; Children's Press, Chicago, IL, USA; 1989.

Clark, Eleanor; *The Legacy of Lord Baden-Powell: The Founder of Scouting*; WinePress Publishing; Enumclaw, WA, USA; 2010.

Drewery, Mary; *Baden-Powell: The Man Who Lived Twice;* National Council, Boy Scouts of Canada; Ottawa, Canada; 1975.

Hillcourt, William with Lady Baden-Powell, Olave; *Baden-Powell: The Two Lives of a Hero*; Boy Scouts of America; 1981.

Schwartz, Sandra and Jeff; *The Scouting Way: A Daily Guide to Living with Scout Values;* The Scouting Way; San Clemente, CA; 2004.

B-P
CONNECT-THE-DOTS

JAMBOREE JUMBLE

ALOSPTR   _____

UTSGCINO FRO
BYOS   _____

OBY CTSUSO   _____

SOTCU WAL   _____

KNFEMGI   _____

LRGI SUDIEG   _____

EB PDRREPAE   _____

DKONHBOA   _____

PSY   _____

THPZICSINEI   _____

DOWO DGAEB   _____

OUSTC HOAT   _____

EERJBMAO   _____

EOHHTBDRORO   _____

FRPSOLNSOAIE
EIOSLRD   _____

LIUNZUID   _____

HFEIC CUSOT   _____

CHIEF SCOUT
CROSSWORD PUZZLE

PUZZLE CLUES

Across

5. Smile and be amiable.
6. Show gratitude.
7. Be prudent.
12. Honor your God, and be devout and respectful.
15. Symbol representing the north point of a compass.
18. Chief Scout of the World.
20. Name of town BP became famous for defending.

Down

1. Be decent and thoughtful.
2. Zulu chief's necklace.
3. Follow the rules.
4. Be polite and respectful.
8. Strive towards purity of thought and deed.
9. Be honest.
10. Ease another's burden.
11. A boy scout pledges to do his best to do his duty to God, country, others, and whom else?
13. South African farmers of Dutch origin.
14. A Zulu chief's name.
16. Be a good friend.
17. BP served as British soldier in this branch of the military.
19. Be courageous.

ANSWER KEY
JAMBOREE JUMBLE

ALOSPTR	Patrols
UTSGCINO FRO BYOS	*Scouting For Boys*
OBY CTSUSO	Boy Scouts
SOTCU WAL	Scout Law
KNFAEMGI	Mafeking
LRGI SUDIEG	Girl Guides
EB PDRREPAE	Be Prepared
DKONHBOA	Handbook
PSY	Spy
THPZICSINEI	Citizenship
DOWO DGAEB	Wood Badge
OUSTC HOAT	Scout Oath
EERJBMAO	Jamboree
EOHHTBDRORO	Brotherhood
FRPSOLNSOAIE	Professional Soldier
EIOSLRD LIUNZUID	Dinizulu
HFEIC CUSOT	Chief Scout

ANSWER KEY
CHIEF SCOUT
CROSSWORD PUZZLE

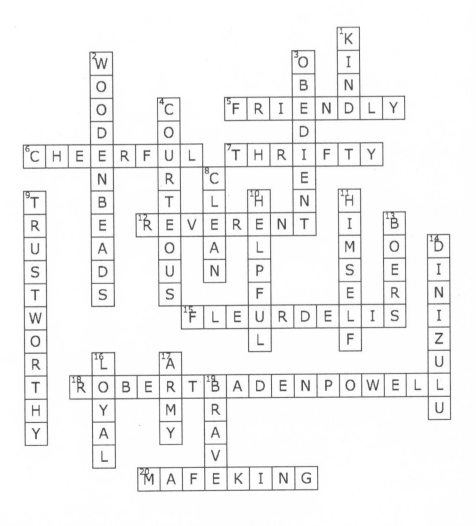

QUOTES BY BADEN-POWELL

❑ "Trust should be the basis of all our moral training."

❑ "We never fail when we try to do our duty. We always fail when we neglect to do it."

❑ "We must change boys from a 'what can I get' to a 'what can I give' attitude."

❑ "The most worth-while thing is to try to put happiness into the lives of others."

❑ "A week of camp life is worth six months of theoretical teaching in the meeting room."

❑ "I have over and over again explained that the purpose of the Boy Scout and Girl Guide Movement is to build men and women as citizens endowed with the three H's – namely,

Health, Happiness, and Helpfulness. The man or woman who succeeds in developing these three attributes has secured the main steps to success this Life."

❑ "The real way to gain happiness is to give it to others."

❑ "A fisherman does not bait his hook with food he likes. He uses food the fish likes. So with boys."

❑ "The man who is blind to the beauties of nature has missed half the pleasure of life."

❑ "Be Prepared." "Be prepared for what?" "Why, for any old thing."

❑ "There is no teaching to compare with example."

❑ "No one can pass through life, any more than he can pass through a bit of country, without leaving tracks behind, and those tracks may often be helpful to those coming after him in finding their way."

❑ "Try to leave this world a little better than you found it and, when your turn comes to die, you can die happy in feeling that at any rate you have not wasted your time but have done your best."

Baden-Powell of Gilwell

TIMELINE OF BADEN-POWELL'S LIFE

1857	Born Robert Stephenson Smyth Powell on February 22, in London, England.
1868-76	Attended Charterhouse School, London, England.
1876	Joined the British Army.
1883	Promoted to Captain at age 26.
1884	Published *Reconnaissance and Scouting*.
1897	Commanded the 5th Dragoon Guards in India. Taught scouting to cavalrymen.
1899	Published *Aids to Scouting*.
1899-1903	Served in the Boer War, South Africa.

1903	Became famous as the Hero of Mafeking.
1903	Became Inspector-General of the military police force in South Africa.
1907	Led campout on Brownsea Island, England.
1908	Published *Scouting For Boys*.
1910	Inspired the founding of the Boys Scouts of America.
1910	Retired from the British Army.
1912	Married Olave St. Clair Soames in Dorset, England.
1912	Published *Handbook For Girl Guides*.
1912	Inspired the founding of the Girl Scouts of America.
1916	Organized Wolf Cub Scouts.
1918	Organized Rover Scouts.

1919   Led first Wood Badge adult Scouter training course at Gilwell, London, England.

1920   Led First Boy Scout Jamboree, London, England. Saluted as, "Chief Scout of the World!"

1929   Honored as Lord Baden-Powell of Gilwell.

1941   Died at age 83 on January 8 in Kenya, Africa.

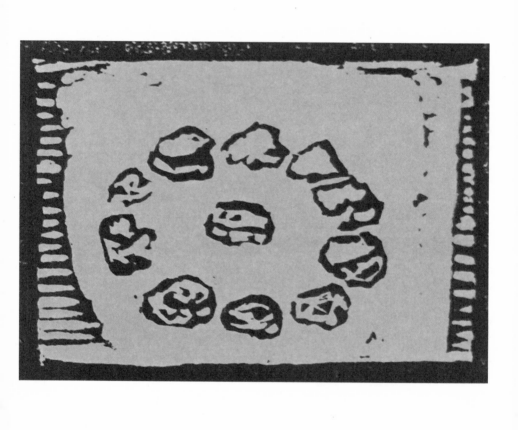